Molly is New

READZONE

ReadZone Books Limited

50 Godfrey Avenue
Twickenham
TW2 7PF
UK

For Alice

First published in this edition 2014

© in this edition ReadZone Books Limited 2014
© in text Nick Turpin 2005
© in illustrations Silvia Raga 2005

Nick Turpin has asserted his right under the Copyright Designs
and Patents Act 1988 to be identified as the author of this work.

Silvia Raga has asserted her right under the Copyright Designs
and Patents Act 1988 to be identified as the illustrator of this work.

Every attempt has been made by the Publisher to secure appropriate
permissions for material reproduced in this book. If there has been any
oversight we will be happy to rectify the situation in future editions or
reprints. Written submissions should be made to the Publisher.

British Library Cataloguing in Publication Data (CIP) is available
for this title.

Printed in Malta by Melita Press

ISBN 978 1 78322 455 5

Visit our website: www.readzonebooks.com

Molly is New

Nick Turpin
and Silvia Raga

READZONE

Molly is new…

...new at school!

She has new shoes
and a new bag.

9

School is big.

So is the teacher!

12

13

Molly draws.

16

She pours…

...and listens...

...and eats lunch.

It's playtime!

Molly falls.

Her knee hurts.

The big teacher
makes it better.

She's nice.

But Mum is nicest!

Did you enjoy this book?

Look out for more *Robins* titles —
first stories in only 50 words!